P O D S

Shawn Winchell

Everybody's
gotta
eat...

PODS

SHAWN WINCHELL

burnt
wick
press

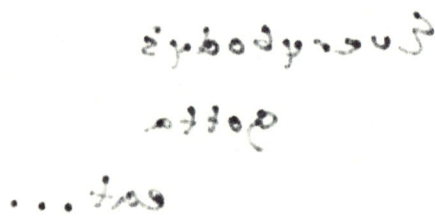

This book is a work of fiction. The names, characters, and events portrayed are the product of the author's imagination. Any resemblance to actual persons, living or dead, events, or localities is entirely coincidental.

ISBN: 979-8-9881396-8-3

Burnt Wick Press

37842 Schulze Rd

Concrete, WA 98237

www.burntwickpress.com

www.shawnwinchell.com

1

Today is the first day of my life.

I've felt this way a few times before—on my wedding day and when Mikey was born—but this time, it's the truth. Don't get me wrong, those other days were important, too. But now that I'm signing the title for my food truck, I finally feel like I can live the life I am supposed to be living.

It's taken years of skimping, picking up extra shifts as a line cook at that shitty restaurant (and even some as a busboy), catering on the side for barely more than the cost of the food. Years of being miserable, going through the motions. And it's taken a toll. My marriage has nearly fallen apart—more than once. Mikey barely knows his own father. He didn't say, "Dad," until he was almost three.

None of that matters anymore, though. Not after today.

I open my wallet and pull out a cashier's check. *Forty-five thousand dollars.* I wanted to pay in cash, but Annalise convinced me not to risk losing the money before I even got to see the truck.

I hand the check to the guy standing next to me and he hands me the keys.

"Good luck," he says.

"Thanks, but I don't need it," I say. "I've been dreaming about this for my whole life."

"So did I. But one thing you don't dream about is the fact that two out of three food trucks go under in three years or less."

"Uh-huh, sure."

He folds the cashier's check and tucks it into the pocket of his red flannel shirt like it's not the grand total of twelve years of my life.

I watch him cross the empty parking lot of the deserted shopping mall and duck into the passenger seat of the only other car here before I climb into my new truck.

"What does he know?" I say as I slip the key into the ignition. The engine sputters and then roars to life. I let the truck—*my* truck—idle, the entire cab vibrating as I take it all in. The combination of burning diesel and the lingering scent of stale oil might very well be the sweetest thing I've ever smelled.

The eight-mile drive back to the tiny starter house that Anna's parents bought us as a wedding present is a blur. I'm on autopilot, creating a mental to-do list instead of paying attention to the road.

By the time I pull up to the curb in front of our house, I'm reasonably certain that I can open for business by the first of next month, especially if my boss's guy in the health department can speed things along for me.

Anna is standing on the porch when I climb out of the truck. I jog across the grass toward her, unable to stop smiling. Even when she cocks her head to the side and puts her hands on her hips.

"So," I say, kissing the corner of her scowl, "what do you think?"

"I *think* you just pissed away our life savings on a piece of shit."

"What are you talking about?" My eyes scan the length of the food truck. Sure, there are some rust spots, and it looks like it was painted with a single coat from a five-dollar can of spray paint. And, yeah, maybe the engine could use a bit of work. Not to mention, all of the kitchen equipment needs to be replaced. "It's perfect."

Anna doesn't look at me once during dinner. She's upset, I get it, but she's not seeing the whole picture. The *potential*. It's all worked out in my head. Hell, I've had it visualized for as long as I can remember. She'll come around, I'm sure of it.

"Daddy, what's that big loud thing you brought home?" Mikey asks as he slurps a foot-long noodle. Little drops of tomato sauce splatter his shirt and the table around his plate.

"That, my boy, is our future," I say.

Anna scoffs as she hands him a napkin and uses her own to wipe the mess off the table.

"Really?" Mikey looks at his mother for confirmation that I'm telling the truth. She rolls her eyes. Mikey laughs.

I pretend not to notice. *She'll come around,* I tell myself. *They both will.*

"You'll see, buddy. By the time I'm through with it, that truck is going to be gorgeous. You'll want nothing more than for it to be yours. And one day, it will be."

I slide my chair back from the table, wiping my mouth before tossing my napkin onto my half-eaten plate of food. There's still an hour or so of daylight left, and I don't want to wait until tomorrow to get started. Plus, I don't want to hear whatever passive-aggressive comment Anna says to Mikey about my truck.

"I'll be out front."

The sun goes down, but I don't want to stop working. There's so much to get done. Our porch light doesn't reach all the way to the street, so I run the extension cord plugged into my power sander underneath the truck to work in the glow of the streetlight.

Time loses all meaning as I sand off the previous owner's logo. I can already see mine going up in its place.

A medley of meat and vegetables being tossed around in a giant wok, surrounded by the perfect name for a stir-fry inspired food truck—

"Micheal Morley!" My fantasy is interrupted by the sharp tone of Anna's voice. She drops the unplugged end of the extension cord and yanks on the cord of the sander, pulling it from my hands as it whines to a stop.

"What the hell?" I say, hopping out of the way of the falling power tool.

"Do you even realize how long you've been out here? Mikey just spent the last hour and a half crying himself to sleep because you promised to read him a bedtime story."

"Ah, shit." I wipe my hands on the back of my thighs. "I'll go do it now. I just gotta get this stuff put away."

"Don't bother. He's asleep. Finally. But your son thinks you hate him"

"That's ridiculous."

"Is it? You're never home. And when you are, all you can think about is your stupid food truck, which you didn't even have until today. Now that you actually have it, do you think that's going to stop? Because I don't."

"Oh, come on. That's not fair." I pick the sander up off the road and wrap the cord around it.

"You want to talk about fair? How about a three-year-old boy who barely knows his own father? All he wants is for you to be part of his life, but every single time, you choose work over him. Does that sound fair to you?"

Anna doesn't stick around long enough for me to give an answer. When she slams the front door closed behind her, I see the blinds move in at least two of the neighboring houses. Fingertips pulling them down just far enough to peek out at the latest drama unfolding at the Morley house.

I open the driver's door of my truck and toss the sander onto the seat. I had been planning to put it in the garage when I roll up the extension cord, but I want my own door to slam. Since everyone's watching anyway, let's really give them a show.

Inside, I duck into Mikey's room. He's sleeping, like Anna said. I don't think he cried himself to sleep, though. Kid looks fine to me. Almost smiling, even.

Mikey's arms are wrapped around a book—*The Little Engine that Could*—and his bedside lamp is still on. I twist the little knob on the lamp and make sure his blanket is tucked snugly around his legs. Before I go, I take the book out of his hands and put it back on the shelf, hoping he won't remember that I didn't read it if he doesn't see it in the morning.

At the end of the hall, our bedroom door is closed. We never close it. Most nights, Mikey wakes up at least once and needs someone—*Anna*—to tuck him back into bed. But it's closed now. And locked.

I take a blanket out of the linen closet and head to the living room.

2

The grand opening. August 30th. A full two days earlier than I hoped for. I suppose I owe that to Anna. After that first late night I spent working on the truck, she didn't make me sleep on the couch again. Actually, she didn't make me do anything.

She cashed in all of her vacation time and took Mikey to stay with her parents while I *thought about my priorities*. The way I see it, my wife and son got to go on a little trip, and I didn't have to worry about prioritizing anything. I'd already given my two-week notice at work, and they were out of town. The only thing left was making sure the truck was ready for the big day.

Today.

I call Anna from the cab of the truck, wanting to tell her the good news. The phone rings twice before the recording of her voice starts to play. She sent me to voicemail. I pin the phone to my ear with my shoulder and drum on the steering wheel while I wait for the beep.

"Anna, hey, voicemail. That's okay. I'm just about to open up the truck for the first time. Was hoping you could bring the boy. Lunch or an early dinner. I don't know how soon you could be on the road. Hell, bring your folks, too. I'm sure they'd be glad to come with. Your mom always says how much she loves my cooking. Anyway, I gotta get started on some prep. I'm parked on 3rd, maybe half a mile east of Main. Right across from the bank. See you soon?" I don't mean for the end of my message to sound like a question, but I can't help it. My entire body feels like it's vibrating. I haven't been this nervous since . . . well, ever.

Slipping my phone into my back pocket, I crawl between the seats into the back of the truck. The clock that I hung on the back of the driver's seat ticks over to 9:00. Time to get started.

I take my apron off the hook on the back door and roll up the window.

Parking across the street from the bank turns out to be a stroke of genius. The people who work there don't have enough time to enjoy their lunch if they walk somewhere else to get it. And everyone who goes to the bank on their own lunch break is out of time to look for something else to eat before they have to get back to work.

From 10:30 until 2:00, I don't even have time to glance at my phone. So, when Anna and Mikey step up to my window at 2:15, I am totally surprised.

"I'm glad you came," I say, leaning forward far enough to awkwardly wrap one arm behind Anna's head. Then I reach over and tousle Mikey's hair (*when did it get so long?*). "Hey, buddy. You hungry?"

He smiles up at me, but before I can ask him what sounds good, a deep voice speaks up from right behind Anna.

"What the hell kind of name is this for a food truck?"

"Nice to see you, too, Mike." It feels weird every time I say my father-in-law's name. Luckily, I've always been Michael, not Mike, but it's still strange.

"*Turn Around and Wok Away.* You're telling your customers to leave before they even see your menu."

"It's wordplay. All food trucks do it."

"Idiotic is what it is." Mike never did have much of an imagination. He's an accountant, a *numbers guy*. Those little booths that pop up in the grocery store during tax season, that's him. Even after all these years, I still am not sure what he does for the rest of the year.

"Would you tell him?" I look toward Anna.

"Sorry, Michael. I think he's got a point. It *does* sound bad . . ."

"Ack," I say, waving an arm and turning back to my wok. "You don't get it."

Anna's dad says something to her. I'm sure he's criticizing something else about my truck, but I can't hear him over the sound of thin-sliced pork frying in sesame oil.

Swirling the wok with one hand, I add the vegetables (strips of bell peppers and onions, carrot coins, fresh garlic, and celery), noodles, and sauce. Anna doesn't like anything spicy and Mikey is a toddler, so I don't give them my personal favorite. Instead, they get a combination of milder seasonings mixed with more oil. Ginger and thyme, with a dash of cinnamon and cumin, and lots of coriander. Still shaking the wok, I drop a handful of diced apple on top. The trick is to add in the apple right at the end. If it cooks for too long, it gets mushy and ruins the whole dish.

I pick the wok up off the burner, still swirling the food, as I lay out four bowls on the counter. Without letting the food settle, I take my tongs and fill the bowls, letting just enough of the excess oil drip back into the wok so the food doesn't taste greasy.

"Here," I say, handing the first bowl to Anna's dad. "Maybe you won't think it's so idiotic after you try this."

I half-expect to come home to an empty house, but Anna's white Corolla is in the driveway and the front door is unlocked when I turn the knob. I toss my keys into the bowl sitting below the light switch.

Anna is in the bathroom with Mikey. Their laughter as he splashes in the tub echoes down

the hallway. Good. I'm glad they are both happy.
I honestly wasn't sure they would be. Anna didn't
say much before they left the food truck.

As I turn into the bathroom, Mikey throws an
entire pitcher of bathwater onto his mother's lap.

"Come on now, buddy. You know the water is
supposed to stay in the tub."

Anna jumps more at the sound of my voice behind her than at the four cups of water soaking
through her jeans. She turns to face me, rising to
her feet.

"Didn't hear you come in," she says. She takes a
hand towel from the rack hanging over the toilet
and blots it on her pants.

"Just got home. So . . . what did you think? We
didn't really get a chance to talk when you came
by earlier."

"Yeah, it was good."

"Good? Of course it was good. I've been perfect-
ing those recipes for years. What did you think of
the truck?"

"You put in a lot of work to get it ready."

"Damn right, I did." I clap my hands together
and squat down next to the bathtub. "How about
you, Mikey? Did you like eating at Daddy's truck
today?"

"Mmhmm, yep." Mikey doesn't look up. In the
water, an epic battle between a two-inch Spiderman toy and an eight-inch-long shark is taking
place, and it looks like Spidey needs some help.

"Man, I wish you could have been there all day.
I couldn't have asked for a better opening."

When I turn away from the tub, Anna is drying her hands with the towel.

"I'm glad it went so well," she says. "Mikey, two more minutes, okay? Then it's time for bed."

"Okay, Mom." As Mikey speaks, Spiderman jumps out of the water, bounces off the edge of the tub, and lands a kick right between the shark's eyes. Mikey tosses the shark to the other end of the bathtub. He stands up and sets the Spiderman toy on the built-in soap tray.

I watch as Mikey pumps two pumps of shampoo into his little hand and begins to wash his hair. Then he picks up the bar of soap and scrubs himself before lying down. The water rises to cover his body and most of his face—only his eyes and nose stay above the water—and he rubs his hands over his skin and through his hair.

I look at Anna, who is grabbing a dry towel for Mikey. "When did he learn how to bathe himself?" I whisper, even though Mikey's ears are still submerged.

"You missed a lot," Anna says, tossing the towel at my head. "Even before you got that truck."

3

After tucking Mikey into bed and finally reading *The Little Engine That Could* to him, I turn off the light and close his bedroom door.

The door to our bedroom is open but dark, and I hear the quiet murmurings of a car insurance commercial coming from the living room.

Anna isn't paying attention to the screen. She's stretched out on the couch, mindlessly scrolling through some social media app on her phone—she's got all of them, and swears each one is for something different, but they're all a waste of time as far as I'm concerned.

She doesn't look up from TickFace—or whatever the hell it's called—when I plop myself into the recliner across from her.

"Mikey's asleep," I say.

"Did you actually read to him this time?" She keeps scrolling.

"Come on, Anna. You say that like I don't care about the kid."

Now she sets the phone face down on her chest. Without the LCD glow, her face disappears into shadows. "Do you? Are you even capable of caring about anything other than that damn truck?"

"Of course I do, but . . ." I pause and let out a sigh. The timing is terrible, but it's the reason I came into the living room. "I'm going to be gone for a few days."

"Yeah, right," Anna scoffs.

"I wouldn't go unless I thought it was for the best. There's this music festival upstate and—"

"Oh my God, you're serious? You really don't care about this family at all, do you?" She sits up, her phone flying off her chest as she does. It bounces off the corner of the table on its way to the floor.

"You don't understand. I have to do this. There's going to be thousands, maybe tens of thousands, of people. All camping out for four days. And every single one will be stoned the whole time. It's a goldmine. I'd have to be an idiot not to go."

Anna leans down to grab her phone. When she picks it up, I can see the spider web from across the room. The entire screen is shattered.

"Great," Anna says when she sees the broken screen. "Whatever, Michael. Do what you want. But don't expect me to be the one to explain to your son why his father chose to miss his entire birthday weekend."

She taps on the phone's screen a few times before setting it on the table and walking out of the room.

After I hear our bedroom door slam shut, I grab the remote and turn off the TV. There used to always be a streak of light that ran the length of the living room from the street at night, but my food truck blocks the view of the streetlamp from the window, so I'm left in the dark. I let my head fall back into the chair.

That could not have gone any worse. I had no idea Mikey's birthday was coming up . . . but I can't miss the festival. Not when I'm just getting started.

The festival goes even better than I hoped. By noon on Monday, I am sold out of everything. Even the fifty-pound bag of white rice that I only bought for people who specifically ask for it. I hate rice with my stir-fry so I don't have it on my menu anywhere. And the best part . . . three-quarters of my customers paid with cash so I don't even have to pay the fee for using my card reader.

As I merge onto the freeway, the sun dips behind a wide blanket of clouds. It's cool outside for Labor Day, so when I reach a straight stretch of road, I unzip the bank deposit bag sitting on the passenger seat and grab a handful of bills. I turn off the air conditioning in the truck and fan myself with my profits.

I can't wait to get home and tell Anna the good news. And I'm sure Mikey will forgive me for missing his birthday when I take him to the toy store at the mall and let him pick out anything he wants.

The four-hour drive back to town goes by in a flash. I usually hate long drives, especially with holiday traffic on the freeway, but nothing could bring me down after the weekend I just had.

In fact, I'm in such a great mood that not even a detour that adds fifteen extra minutes to my drive after sitting at a dead stop for half an hour brings me down.

I glance out the window as the truck crawls past a cop who must have drawn the short straw. He is standing in front of a line of cones strung together with yellow crime scene tape waving everyone down an unpaved side road. Before now, I'd never actually seen that tape in person. I thought they only used it in Hollywood.

Two blocks behind the traffic cop, there is a row of cars (four police cruisers, an ambulance, a fire truck, and a black Charger that must be an unmarked cop car). The only other vehicle is a small white car parked in front of a fire hydrant. Seems odd that they'd do all of this if there wasn't a big wreck—a fatality or head-on collision or something—but the car looks fine to me. I can't see any cones farther down the street so they must have a pretty big area blocked off. There is a small group of police officers squatting around something on the road. The rest of them are standing around by their cars.

If I had any food left, I'd pull over and open the window. A bunch of bored cops would make great customers. Maybe next time.

"Anna?" I call out after unlocking the house even though her car isn't in the driveway. "Anna, are you home? I've got good news."

When the only response is the sound of my keys landing in the bowl by the door, I slide my phone out of my pocket.

No missed calls. No texts.

I suppose I shouldn't be surprised. She takes Mikey out of the house every chance she gets.

I try to call her but it goes to her voicemail without ringing. I see why when I go into the kitchen to grab a beer from the fridge. She hasn't replaced her phone yet, and the one with the shattered screen is sitting on the counter in front of the microwave.

"Oh well," I say, popping the tab on a can of Coors Light. I sip the beer as I count the money in my deposit bag for the fourth time today.

When I finish the beer and she still isn't home, I get into the shower to wash the layer of oil off my face and the secondhand weed smell off of my skin.

I stand in the hot water for almost half an hour, but there's still no sign of Anna or Mikey when I finish. I take another beer out of the fridge.

Sitting on the couch, I think I'll find some dumb movie with a bunch of explosions and cheesy catchphrases to pass the time until they get home and I can give them the good news. I open the beer with one hand as I lean forward to grab the remote off the table.

There is a slip of paper beneath the remote. A note. One sentence written in Sharpie.

Don't bother trying to find us until
you get your priorities straight.

The can drops from my hand, turning into a fountain of white foam as it hits the hardwood floor.

I pick up the note and read it again. And again.

And then I crumple it into a ball and shove it into my pocket as I head for the door.

"The hell with this," I say as I grab my keys out of the bowl.

4

Thankfully, my distributor takes will-call orders on top of their normal deliveries. I'll be damned if I'm going to sit in that empty house when there's a perfectly good crime scene filled with hungry cops waiting for me—not to mention the lookie-loos who are bound to show up at some point.

It's ten to six when I get back to the traffic cop. When I pull out of the line of traffic to park, he takes a step toward me with his arms up like he is going to wave me off, but he stops and puts one hand on his stomach. The cop looks over his shoulder and pats the seat of his pants with his other hand. And then he pulls out his wallet.

Got him, I think as I set the parking brake and step between the seats into my kitchen. By the time I tie my apron and crank open the window, he is standing right outside my truck.

"I'm starving," he says, "what's good?"

With a smile, I start heating the wok and suggest the number two.

"Hey guys, food truck," he shouts, jogging back toward the crime scene tape. "Who needs a bite?"

By the time I finish Traffic Cop's order, there are six others standing in line. The rest are trying to look busy while stealing glances at my window. It's just about dinnertime and who knows how long they've been out here.

Most of the officers step back and talk amongst themselves while they wait for their food, but one of them lingers at the window. This is the only part of the job that I could do without. I *hate* small talk. But . . . I also hate feeling like someone is staring at me—especially when that someone has a gun strapped to their waist.

"So," I say, shaking two of the three woks sizzling in front of me, "what happened? Are you allowed to tell me or is it some sort of secret investigation?"

The cop breathes in the scent of the seasonings as I drizzle sauce into each of the woks and I hear his stomach growl. One corner of my mouth turns up as I add a little extra sauce, just to mess with him. His tongue darts across his upper lip before he answers, wetting the ends of his mustache hairs. "Nah, it's no big secret. Truth be told, we don't know what happened. If you ask me, I don't think it's even a crime scene."

"Really? How do you mean?" I ask, now legitimately interested in this conversation.

"No one saw anything. There are no signs of struggle anywhere that we can find. Just an abandoned car that seems like it runs just fine and one shoe in the middle of the street that could have come from anywhere."

"Huh, that does sound a bit odd." I set the first three bowls on the counter. "Order up," I shout to the other cops.

"It's not odd," says a wet-sounding voice from behind my truck.

I didn't realize anyone else was close enough to hear, but he must've been there at least long enough to know what we were talking about. The man steps around the back of the truck and up to the window. His head barely rises above the bottom of my window, so he can't be much more than five feet tall. His long gray hair hangs down from beneath a flannel baseball cap in greasy spirals and he has a beard that looks like the frayed end of a rope. An oversized black tee with *I KNOW THE TRUTH* printed in white block letters across the chest hangs to his knees.

"Ah," says the cop, waving a hand dismissively at the man, "what do you know?"

The man lets out a laugh, pointing at his shirt. "I know the truth, man."

The man's name is William McGallagher.

"But most people call me Scruff," he says.

When Scruff didn't walk away from my truck, the cop I'd been talking to did. He's back on the other side of the yellow tape with the other cops.

"Okay *Scruff*," I say, trying not to laugh, "if you know the truth, then what is it?"

"Aliens."

I can't hold it in any longer. I let out a bark of laughter, but when I lean down to hand Scruff's order to him, his face is straight. He doesn't get mad or defensive—something tells me he's used to getting laughed at—he just takes his food and watches me.

"Sorry. I'm sorry," I say, trying to get it together.

"You done?" Scruff says, his eyes scanning every inch of my face.

"Yeah, yeah . . . yes, I'm done. I didn't mean to laugh, but aliens? You can't be serious."

"Dead serious." He pauses to slurp a noodle that slipped from his fork into his beard and it takes everything I have to keep from bursting into laughter again. "It's been happening for at least fifteen years. Probably longer, but I can't confirm any more than that. And it's becoming more frequent."

"What is?"

"Targeted alien abductions. They are planning something big and it's happening soon. It's the only logical explanation."

"Buddy, I don't know how logical it is, but if you say it's aliens, I guess I'll take your word for it."

"You don't have to," he says. "I can prove it."

"I'm sure you can, but I've got to finish cleaning up here. Good to meet you, Scruff." I start turning the crank to lower the window before he can say anything. It feels like he was building toward a big reveal and I'm too tired to pretend to care about that tonight.

It doesn't take long to get everything washed and put away. Cleaning up after eight orders is practically nothing after spending the weekend at the music festival. And I'm glad. I wasn't lying when I told Scruff I was tired. All I want to do now is head home, grab a beer, and pass out in front of the TV so I don't have to remember that my wife left me and took our son with her.

A quick double knock on the other side of the closed serving window stops me before I can step between the seats into the cab of the truck. I turn back and slowly roll up the window.

"Hey man, I thought I told you—"

"Are you Michael Morley?" It's not Scruff who knocked like I thought. It's the cop I was talking to before he showed up.

"Yeah . . . what's going on?"

"Do you know where your wife is?"

My hand drops to my side, patting the crumpled note from Anna inside my pocket. Probably best not to mention that until I know what he wants.

"I haven't seen her in a few days. Been out of town. If I had to guess, I'd say she's probably at home with our son. Which is where I'd like to be. So if you don't mind . . ." I start to reach for the handle to close the window, but the cop blocks my hand with the notepad he's holding.

"Does she own a white Corolla?"

"*We* do," I say. "But I think it's registered in her name, yeah. What's this all about?"

"Well, sir, we ran the plates on the abandoned car over there and got her name. And the only

23

other vehicle registered with the same address is this food truck."

"That's Anna's car over there? Where is my wife?"

"You mentioned that you have a son," the cop continues, ignoring my questions. "Does this shoe belong to him?"

He sets a plastic bag on the counter with a size eight toddler sneaker inside it.

"I . . . I really don't know. It could. What happened to Anna? Where's Mikey?"

"That's what we are trying to figure out." The cop takes the evidence bag off the counter and replaces it with a business card. "If you think of anything we ought to know, or if you hear from your wife, give us a call."

I pick up the card without looking at it. My eyes stay glued to the white car down the street—on the other side of the crime scene tape—Anna's car.

I'm not sure how long I stare, but by the time I close the window and start the truck, it's dark outside and all of the cop cars are long gone.

5

Back at home, I grab a beer and sit on the couch.

They're gone

I try not to think about Anna and Mikey—

They're really gone

—or what that Scruff guy thinks happened to them.

Targeted alien abductions

I take a large sip from the can and shake my head.

"He doesn't know anything," I say to my reflection in the dark television screen. "That guy is nuts."

Taking another sip, I reach for the remote. Maybe there's something decent on that can distract me for a while.

As the screen comes to life, I notice the logo in the bottom right corner. *SyFy*.

A movie is playing. I'm not sure which one until I see a young Will Smith dragging an alien across a desert.

"Nope." I change the channel.

Here's another movie channel. This one looks promising. Harrison Ford with a fedora is usually a good sign. Except, here comes Shia LaBeouf. More aliens . . . great.

The next channel is playing a cartoon. An old guy and a kid get into a car that's not a car and fly off into space.

Next is a documentary on the History Channel. That's not usually my thing, but I'll give it a shot. It's showing images of the pyramids in Egypt, so it could be interesting. Now the show cuts to a close-up of a guy with crazy hair. He brings both of his hands up and says one word. "Aliens."

"You've got to be kidding," I say, pushing the power button on the remote and throwing it at the TV.

The crumpled scrap of paper that Anna wrote her goodbye note on is still in my pocket. I lay it on the coffee table and finish my beer so I can use the can like a rolling pin to smooth it out.

And then I just stare at the words.

A simple message. Concise.

And what did I do when I read those words for the first time?

Exactly what she expected me to. I chose the food truck over my family.

Now they're gone. Even the cops have no idea where they went.

I've spent everything I have on that truck. And it's cost me everything I had.

And the worst part is . . . tonight, I don't give a shit about it.

I just want my family.

I'm still staring at the note—the last little piece of Anna I have left—when the sunrise lights up the living room.

I've only stood up from the couch once, to get more beer, and that was hours ago. I don't want to get up again, but my bladder is screaming.

When I get to the bathroom, I close the door. Maybe if I act like they're still here, they won't really be gone.

After unzipping my pants, I slide my phone out of my pocket and press the button on the side. Anna is just about the only person I talk to unless it's about something to do with work, so it takes a couple of seconds for me to realize that there is a voicemail.

I tap on the notification and set the phone on the counter.

You son of a bitch. Anna's dad, pleasant guy. *They should have been here hours ago. Let me guess, she told you they were leaving and you just couldn't have that, could you? What the hell did you do to my daughter? And my grandson?*

I shake off and pick up the phone.

Mike answers before the first ring is finished.

"If you did anything to them, I swear to God—"

"Take it easy, Mike. I haven't seen them. They were already gone when I got home from the festival yesterday. I don't know what happened."

I know the truth, man.

"Then where are they? Why isn't she answering her phone?"

I have to hold the phone away from my ear as Mike screams at me. Is that what I should be doing? Accusing people of doing something to my family and screaming at anyone who will listen?

"Didn't the cops call you?" *Do they call the parents if they talk to the husband?*

"Cops? Why would the cops call?"

"They found her car. And maybe Mikey's shoe. There's no sign of an accident or anything. It looks like they ditched the car right before the freeway."

"Why? Why . . . why would Anna do that?"

"I don't know, Mike. She watched a lot of those true crime shows. Isn't that something they do when they don't want to be found?"

"She's not a criminal, you idiot. She was running away from her piece of shit husband, not the FBI."

"Look, Mike, it's been a long night. Like you said, my wife took my son and left me. I haven't slept. And, honestly, I really don't want to be having this conversation. Especially with you."

Mike growls—*actually* growls—at me, but I don't hear any more of his reply before I hang up the phone.

I open the bathroom door with a smile on my face and turn toward the bedroom.

My eyes close as my body falls onto the mattress and fall asleep to the sound of my phone buzzing on the counter in the bathroom.

I don't normally remember my dreams, but I don't think I'll ever forget this one.

I'm driving around town, looking for a good corner to park my truck on for the day. But there aren't any other cars on the road. No people walking on the sidewalks. The entire city is deserted, except for me and my food truck.

When I turn onto Fifth Street, I see the reason why. Several orange cones are blocking the road, tied together with yellow crime scene tape. On the other side, a crowd has formed, trying to sneak a peek at whatever the police don't want them to see. The cop who asked me about Anna stands between the onlookers and the cones, hands held out in front of him. *Stay back. Nothing to see here.*

For a moment, I consider pulling up to the yellow tape and opening up there—big crowds are always full of hungry people—but before I even know that I've made a decision, I turn onto Main and pull over in front of a fire hydrant.

As far as I can tell, I'm the only person on this side of the crime scene tape. I slip between the seats and tie on my apron anyway. And then I crank open the service window.

By the time the window is all the way open, I have a line of at least ten customers waiting to place their orders.

But they aren't human.

They look like people . . . sort of. Their bodies are human-shaped. But most of them have two long slits above their mouths instead of a nose. And their eyes are all way too big. Half have green skin, some gray, and a couple are blue.

Every alien in line is pushing their way as close to the window as they can, waving cash above their head and shouting their order at me. They aren't ordering in English, though. Instead of words, all I hear is a chorus of clicks and hums.

Clicks and hums that, somehow, I understand.

"Hold on, hold on," I say to them as I fire up my burners. "One at a time."

I proceed to make each of them exactly what they ask for, until the final customer. I don't have any meat left on the counter so I have to grab more out of the cooler.

I flip open the lid and grab a knife to slice some meat. There's only one order left to make, but I want to make sure I'm ready in case anyone wants seconds, so I cut off an entire leg and begin slicing.

When I reach the end of the leg, something much tougher than meat stops my blade. I'd only been halfway paying attention to what I was doing—I was watching my customers enjoy their meals like I always do—and when I look down I see the problem.

My knife is stuck in the sole of a sneaker the size of my fist.

I raise the blade until it is right in front of my face.

"This shouldn't be here," I say, rotating the knife to look at the shoe.

Click. Hum. Click-click. The only alien without any food slaps the side of my truck with a three-fingered hand.

"Yeah, all right, calm down," I say, my attention snapping back to the task at hand. "I'm working on it."

I take a handful of freshly sliced meat and drop it into the hot oil waiting in the wok.

The alien turns its head away from the truck and watches the others eat.

"Jesus, it's always the same," I say under my breath as I add the vegetables to the order. "Good food takes time. Nobody gets that anymore."

It takes a few minutes of staring at my ceiling when I wake up before I'm aware that I am awake.

That dream felt so real. It's crazy. I know that now. But it didn't *feel* crazy. That's the craziest thing about it.

I might have stayed in bed thinking about it for the rest of the day if not for the pounding at my door.

The alarm clock on the nightstand reads *8:24.* An hour and a half is not enough sleep. I roll onto my side and fold a pillow over my ear. The pounding gets louder.

"Come on, man. I can't leave until you sign for this, and I've got a lot more stops to make this morning," someone shouts from the other side of the front door. He stops knocking so I unfold the pillow and close my eyes.

Just as I'm about to drift off to sleep again, the doorbell starts to ring. And ring and ring and ring and ring.

"Fine, I'm coming." I rub my eyes and try to stifle a yawn as I walk down the hall toward the door.

"Here," the delivery man says when I open the door. He shoves a clipboard and pen into my hands. "Where do you want it?"

"I don't care," I say through a yawn. "Here's fine, I guess."

"Great." He rips the clipboard away as soon as I finish signing, clearly agitated. Then, through gritted teeth, he says, "Have a nice day."

I'm still standing in the open doorway when he drives off.

Stacked on the porch is my weekly delivery. Seven boxes of pork, beef, chicken, and produce. I yawn and grab the truck keys out of the bowl by the door.

Bending over to pick up one of the boxes, I start to yawn again and lose my balance. I catch myself on the box of beef and look toward the road. My truck is parked *so* far away.

I just want to go back to bed. I'm sure this stuff won't spoil before I wake up.

Dropping the keys back into the bowl, I close the door and go back to bed.

6

On my way back to the bed, I close all of the blinds. It's not so bad yet, but as soon as the sun gets a little higher, the glare would make it impossible to stay asleep. On an ordinary day, I would also make sure to plug in my phone. There's nothing ordinary about today, though. I set it to silent and leave it on top of the dresser before crawling into bed.

It's dark outside by the time I wake up to pee, so I get back in bed after I wash my hands. I think about checking my phone, but even if Anna and Mikey turned up somewhere, she wouldn't call. That was the whole point of leaving the note, wasn't it? Missing or not, they're gone.

I let my body fall onto the mattress and curl up under the comforter.

I don't wake up again until morning. A dreamless sleep this time.

Even after nearly twenty-four hours in bed, I still feel like I need more sleep. When I try to swallow, my throat fights back, so I force myself to get up.

There is a glass on the counter next to the sink in the kitchen. I can't remember what had been in it, but it looks clean. I turn on the tap and raise the glass to my nose. I barely have to inhale before the sour stench of fermented orange juice burns my nostrils. I drop the glass into the sink and turn off the faucet. There's a fresh six pack in the fridge that will help my throat just as much as a glass of water. Might make it easier to fall back to sleep, too.

I finish one of the cans on my way back to the bedroom and crack another as I toss the empty toward my closet door.

They should still be here. It's Anna's fault they're missing. Everything I've done has been for us. But she never got it. She didn't want *to get it. She wanted to cut and run and look what that got them.*

I try to reassure myself that there was nothing I could have done to change what happened to them as I tip the can up, letting my head fall back into my pillow as I finish the beer.

I squeeze the empty can, folding it into an hour-glass shape before throwing it across the room. I set the remainder of the six pack on the pillow next to me—*Anna's pillow*—and close my eyes.

I have the alien dream again. This time, instead of a leg wearing one of Mikey's shoes, when I run out of meat, I slice up an arm. The fingers on the hand look freshly manicured with Anna's favorite color of nail polish, and her wedding band is on the ring finger.

But the most disturbing thing about the dream is that it doesn't feel disturbing at all. It doesn't feel like anything other than a normal day in the truck.

Anna would probably try to tell me that it's my subconscious manifesting my guilt about what happened to them in the only way to get my attention. Or some bullshit like that.

The thing is, it's not my fault. So why should I feel guilty? She's the one who chose to leave. All I was doing was trying to give our family a good life.

I did it all for them.

Didn't I?

The next few days (*weeks?*) are more of the same.

Sleep, pee, sleep, beer, sleep.

I don't even know what day it is anymore. Not that it matters. Without my family to take care of, there's no point in even getting out of bed.

Who cares if I'm drinking this beer at seven in the morning on a Thursday or at dinnertime on Saturday?

Not Anna.

Not Mikey.

And sure as hell not me.

A knock at the door interrupts my trip back to bed with a couple of fresh beers.

I consider ignoring it, but my curiosity gets the better of me.

As soon as I open the door, I wish I hadn't.

The traffic cop from the crime scene is standing on my porch with one hand shooing flies away from his head and the other plugging his nose.

"Mr. Morley," he says, his voice made nasally by his pinched nostrils. "We've received some calls—"

"You found them? Are they okay? Where are they?" I let the beers drop from my hands and throw my arms around the police officer.

He unplugs his nose and pushes my arms away from him.

"No, we have no new information about your wife and son." He takes a step back and makes a gagging sound before pinching his nose again. "The calls were from some of your neighbors. They've been complaining about a strange smell coming from your house." He dips his head to the side of the porch.

A stack of boxes, the cardboard now mostly black instead of light brown, is collapsing in on itself.

"Ah, shit. I completely forgot. I had an early delivery and went back to bed. I meant to put them in the truck when I woke up."

The cop raises an eyebrow. "How long did you go back to sleep for?"

"Depends," I say. "What day is it?"

"The twenty-eighth."

"It's been a while." My last delivery came on the fifth.

"Whatever. Just get it cleaned up, all right? This is disgusting. And I *really* don't want to come back if it keeps getting worse."

"Yeah, sure thing." How can it already be the end of the month? There's no way I've been in bed for three weeks.

The cop gets into his car but doesn't pull away from the curb. I guess he wants me to do it now.

The smell doesn't bother me as much as it does him—and apparently several of my neighbors. Then again, the only times I've gotten out of bed in twenty-four days are a few quick trips to the bathroom or the fridge. I tilt my chin toward one of my armpits and sniff. And I honestly don't smell much different than the pile of rotting meat and vegetables on my porch.

It's the slimy feeling that gets me. My shoulders tense up and I have to fight off a shiver as soon as I feel it.

When I pick up the top box, I can feel the bottom start to give out. I pull it tight to my stomach and raise my thigh to try to keep the soggy cardboard together. I might not notice the smell, but I know I don't want to deal with cleaning it off my porch if the box falls apart.

Once I am confident that I can move without the box spilling its guts, I look up at the street. The cop is still there, watching.

I shift the weight of the box to my hip and raise a hand toward him with a smile.

"I'm doing it," I say under my breath, trying not to let my lips move. "You can go now." I flick my wrist back and forth, hoping the wave will get my point across.

He starts the car but doesn't shift into drive until the first box is in my trash bin and the second is in my hands.

The sunlight burns my eyes. I can feel my brain pulsing along with my heartbeat inside my skull. I want to go back to bed.

But I also don't want to have to come back outside anytime soon—and I'm already halfway there—so I walk to the end of the driveway and open the mailbox.

It is full enough that the mailman had to start cramming envelopes in to make them fit. Almost every piece of mail is folded or bent, and a few are wedged in tight enough that it takes both hands to pull them free.

I grab as much as I can carry, leaving the mail-box about a quarter full. I don't plan on making a second trip, but at least now there's room for whatever else comes before I decide to brave the outdoors again.

A couple of grocery store circulars slip out of my grasp on my way back to the house. I don't care enough to bend down to pick them up, though. And that shouldn't be enough of a reason for my neighbors to call the police on me again . . . I hope.

A cloud drifts in front of the sun and the pres-sure behind my eyes eases a bit. I pick up the pace. I want to be back inside long before my front yard is back in direct sunlight.

7

B lack dots dance around in front of my eyes. I'm trying to flip through the huge stack of mail sitting on my kitchen table, but it's taking everything I've got just to stay on my feet.

I don't even bother looking for a glass. I stick my head directly under the faucet and turn on the water.

Three and a half weeks, I think as I straighten up and wipe a sweat-stained sleeve across my mouth.

Shaking my head, I cross the kitchen and open the fridge. *When was the last time I ate? Have I eaten* anything *since they left?* I must have, but I can't remember what—or when.

Most of the food in the refrigerator looks to be well on its way to joining the mold party currently taking place in the trash bin outside.

That's fine by me. Cooking is the last thing I feel like doing.

I check the freezer. There's not much there—I always insisted on cooking fresh meals—but there are a few dino nuggets left in a plastic bag tucked behind the ice tray.

I have to wipe a thin layer of frost off of the bag to read the directions before putting them into the microwave.

A little over a minute later, the microwave beeps. My stomach tightens as the smell of the nuggets wafts through the kitchen.

Without waiting for it to cool off, I shove a tyrannosaurus into my mouth. It burns my tongue, but I don't care. I think I even let out a moan while I chew.

"Wherever you are, Anna, thank you for not listening when I said these were garbage that we shouldn't feed our son."

When my plate is empty, I put another serving into the microwave and sit down at the table. I still have some black spots in my vision, but there are fewer than before, and they aren't moving as quickly. I begin to leaf through the mail while I wait for my nuggets to finish cooking.

A lot of it is junk, but several of the envelopes—more than I'd like—are bills that are due this week or already late. Turns out there's a downside to spending the better part of a month in bed.

The microwave beeps and nothing else matters. I pull the garbage can over from the corner and slide the pile of mail into it, bills and all.

With a belly full of dinosaur-shaped processed meat, I feel a bit more human.

I turn on the shower and go into the bedroom while the water warms up. Before taking off my clothes, I plug in my phone and power it up. Because that's what humans do, right? We always have to check our phones.

As soon as my background image shows on the screen—Anna, holding Mikey on her hip, standing next to me in front of the food truck on the morning after I bought it—it starts to beep.

A dozen voicemails.

All from Mike.

And I make the mistake of listening to each one.

The first couple are pretty much the same as the conversation we had the morning after they disappeared. But after that, each one is darker and more aggressive than the last.

He calls me a worthless sack of shit.

He says they don't deserve whatever happened to them, but I do.

He thinks Anna would have been able to really make something of herself if she'd never met me. She always had big dreams, he says, until the day we got married.

He says that if anyone has a reason to fake a disappearance, it's her. And he's okay with never seeing his daughter or grandson again if it means they got away from me.

He thinks the world would be better off without me in it and that I should go ahead and do everyone a favor by killing myself.

And by the time I finish listening to all of the messages, I think I agree.

It's not a decision I come to lightly. I think a part of me has been considering it since that very first night. I mean, how else could I have stayed in bed *that* long without even noticing? The only way that happens is if my mind, even subconsciously, is working out something big. Huge. Life-altering *(ending)*.

I know just how to do it, too.

Last spring, our dryer crapped out on us. It pissed me off at the time, especially when Anna insisted on getting a top-of-the-line replacement. I was in the homestretch, with almost enough money set aside to start shopping around for a truck. As far as I was concerned, we should have been looking online for someone who had one they wanted to give away. But now, as I make my way into the back of the laundry room, I have a different opinion.

The exhaust hose from the old dryer is on the top shelf behind the washing machine. If Anna had listened to me, our replacement dryer wouldn't have come with an installation kit that included a new hose, and my plan wouldn't work.

"Thank you, Anna," I say as I stretch up onto my toes and swipe my fingers at the hose until it rolls off the shelf toward me.

I tuck the exhaust hose under my arm and head for the garage, expecting to have a bit of cleaning to do before I can get down to it.

When I open the door and turn on the light, I don't believe what I see. It's like Anna knew exactly what I would decide to do. The garage is spotless. I can't remember ever seeing it this clean except for maybe on the day we first moved into the house.

"Well, that was easy." My words echo through the empty garage as I set the hose down beneath the light switch and slap the button on the wall.

I pat my pockets, making sure I have the keys to the food truck, as the garage door slowly rises. I don't want to wait—if it takes too long, I might lose my nerve—so as soon as the bottom of the door is chest-high, I duck under and run out to the truck.

I back the food truck into the garage and leave it running.

"If I were a hose clamp," I mutter as I get out and start rummaging through drawers and shelves. I know I have some, I just don't know where Anna put them. I'm not used to the garage being organized. The last place I remember seeing them was on top of an oil drip pan next to my belt sander.

I find the belt sander inside a rolling cabinet with my other power tools. The drip pan is tucked into the front corner of the garage. And the hose clamps are . . .

"Got 'em," I shout, pumping my fist. They are in a drawer behind an old silverware tray filled with screws and bolts, all sorted by size. *When did she have time to do all of this?*

I take a clamp that will fit around the dryer hose and turn around. The garage door is still open. At the end of the driveway, I see our neighbor with her yappy little dog staring at me. *Shit.*

I raise my hand up over my head. "Hi there, Mrs. Jacobs. Just doing some maintenance on my truck. Sorry if I scared your pup." I force myself to smile even though I can practically hear the judgement in the look she's giving me.

Mrs. Jacobs shakes her head without saying anything and tugs on the leash to get her dog to follow her across the street. As soon as her back is turned, I hit the button to close the garage door. Can't afford any more interruptions.

I have everything I need now and I'm moving quickly. I haven't been this motivated to do anything that wasn't related to my food truck in a long time.

I slip the hose from the dryer over the tip of the exhaust pipe and tighten the hose clamp. Once it's secure, I open the back door of the truck and toss the other end of the hose inside.

I climb into the truck and close the door as much as I can, tying one end of my apron to the handle and the other to one of the shelves to keep it there.

Already, I can smell the exhaust spreading throughout the back of the truck, but the door can't close all the way because of the hose. I unroll a few trash bags and duct tape them over the gap.

"I think that about does it," I say, clapping my hands together like I just accomplished something impressive. Then I look around the interior of my truck. I don't know why. I know the only place to sit is up in the cab.

Plopping down in the driver's seat, I reach back for the seatbelt—habit—and take out my phone, planning to doom scroll (ha-ha) while I wait for the end. I change my mind when it starts to buzz in my hand and Mike's name pops up on the screen.

I toss the phone into the back of the truck and look at the exhaust hose, trying to *see* how much carbon monoxide has made its way in so far.

"How long is this supposed to take?" I shake my head and reach for the radio dial.

My hands are trembling, but maybe some music will help.

The exhaust stench grows stronger.

My eyelids begin to droop.

I recline the seat back as far as I can and put my hands behind my head.

A Lynyrd Skynyrd song winds down.

I *do* start to feel as free as a bird.

I let my eyes close, imagining Anna standing on the front porch as I drive up to the house after that damn music festival. Mikey is on her hip, sucking on something that I'm sure I told her I didn't think we should let him eat.

My cheeks go numb, but I still feel the corners of my mouth turn up.

And then the song is interrupted by three sharp alarm blasts.

An AMBER Alert.

A five-year-old child is missing. Last seen with her mother. Their car was found abandoned on the side of the road about four miles from their home.

My eyes shoot open. I lean forward and turn up the volume to listen to the rest of the message.

I unbuckle my seatbelt and jump into the back of the truck to kick the exhaust hose out and close the door.

That sounds a lot like what happened to Anna and Mikey . . . and it happened less than an hour and a half away.

8

Even driving with both windows down on the freeway, it takes almost forty-five minutes for the smell of exhaust to clear out of the food truck. Now that it has, my head feels like it's pounding harder than ever. And my stomach, not wanting to be shown up, cramps and gurgles.

There are a couple of golden arches rising up over the next off-ramp, so I whip over into the right lane and take the exit.

In the drive-thru, I stare at the menu board for several minutes. I haven't eaten at McDonald's since I was a kid. The voice in the speaker tells me to order when I'm ready. When I don't immediately respond with a combo number, the speaker crackles and the voice repeats itself.

"Yeah, I heard you. I'm looking at the menu," I say.

The teenager on the other end of that speaker doesn't turn off his headset fast enough. I catch the beginning of his scoff before the sound cuts out. Getting scoffed at in a McDonald's drive-thru . . . I bet Anna's dad would hate to know he's missing this.

I'm trying to decide what I want to order—I can't tell what is on anything when there's just a name and a picture—when the voice speaks up again.

"Please place your order, sir."

"I said I'm looking. Maybe I'd be able to decide if this menu wasn't *bullshit*." I don't mean for my voice to sound so sharp, but between my head, my stomach, and those damn pictures, I can't help it.

"Sir, I'm going to have to ask you to pull forward and leave." A new voice, older. Must be the manager.

"No, please, look, I'm just having a tough time reading this menu. Can I just get some chicken nuggets?"

A long pause. Then the older voice says, "Six, ten, or twenty?"

My mouth actually falls open. The bag of Mikey's dino nuggets said a serving was only four.

"Twenty? I'll take the twenty," I say, wiping drool from the corner of my lips.

"Would you like fries with that?"

I'm still licking the salty grease off my fingertips when I reach the location mentioned in the AMBER Alert.

It's a different town. The streets have different names and are lined with pines instead of maples. But it looks exactly the same.

Police tape blocks off a huge area and all of the cops are standing around with no idea what they are supposed to be doing.

No one is directing traffic, though.

I pull over alongside the yellow tape and set the parking brake.

"Okay, I'm here," I say as I turn the volume knob on the radio down to zero. "Now what?"

My fingers drum on the steering wheel while I stretch my neck toward the windshield and look around the crime scene.

After a couple of minutes, one of the cops notices me. He elbows his partner and points. The other officer shrugs and turns his back to me. Glad to see I'm not the only one who isn't interested in his job anymore.

Thump, thump, thump!

The sound of someone's fist beating against the serving window echoes throughout the mostly empty food truck. I jump, causing the sun visor to karate chop the back of my neck. Sucking teeth and rubbing my neck, I lean over to check the passenger-side mirror.

"You've got to be kidding," I say as I crawl between the seats to open the serving window.

"Always good to see a newbie joining the fight," Scruff says as soon as the window opens far enough for him to see my face.

"What fight?"

"The fight against all the lies *they* want us to believe."

"I'm not joining anything. I don't even know what I'm doing here."

"Whatever you say, man." Scruff winks and gives me a thumbs-up. "Hey, you got any more of those noodles?"

Even after I tell Scruff that I don't have any food to make for him, he sticks around. If I have to guess, I'd say he isn't used to having anyone to talk to whenever he shows up at the scene of a disappearance. Not that I'm actually talking to him. It's more like he's talking and I'm nodding along, saying things like "sure," and "right," every so often. I couldn't even say what it is I'm agreeing with. I'm not really listening to him. He doesn't seem to notice.

"Hey, so what's the deal with showing up at these places? Do they ever tell you anything?" I ask when I notice two of the cops start walking toward us.

Scruff laughs. "What do you think? Nah, they take one look at me and write me off as crazy. Not that they'd ever admit it."

"Can you blame them?" I run my eyes from Scruff's face down to his holey sneakers and back. "It's not like you're trying very hard to hide it."

"That's 'cause I got nothing to hide! Not like them!" He waves his arm in the general direction of the crime scene, his face turning a shade of red I've only ever seen in that jumbo box of crayons.

"Whoa, settle down. I didn't mean anything by it. I'm just saying, you have a certain . . . *look*. Maybe you fit one of those profile things they always talk about in those cop shows."

"Sure, yeah, maybe." Now Scruff is the one responding without hearing. He turns to the cops ducking under the yellow tape. "Don't tell me you've come to your senses. You here to finally come clean about what's really going on?"

"Ha! You wish, nutball. We came over because it's been a long day. Some of us are getting pretty hungry." The officer turns away from Scruff and looks up at my window. He tips his hat up to get a better look at the menu behind me. "Do you—"

I don't hear anything else. Not after I see his face.

He has two long slits where his nose should be.

His eyes are pitch black and shaped like upside-down eggs, each bigger than my fist.

Where his mouth should be, there is only a thumb-sized, toothless hole.

But—somehow—between the nose slits and mouth hole, he has a thick, blonde mustache.

Oh, and his skin isn't skin-colored . . . it's blue.

Am I really seeing this? Is Scruff? If this is real, how is he not freaking out right now?

I press the heels of my palms into my eyes and rub.

When my hands move away from my face, the cop is just a cop. Not a blue-skinned alien.

"I'm sorry, what did you say?"

"Got anything spicy?"

I shake my head. "Sorry. No food."

51

A deep wrinkle creases the cop's forehead and he raises an eyebrow that is almost as full as his mustache—which he strokes a couple of times before opening his mouth to respond.

His partner grabs him by the elbow and tugs. "C'mon Rog, it's not worth it. We'll just send someone for subs."

The second cop lifts the crime scene tape so Rog can walk under without ducking.

I see Rog shaking his head and hear what he is muttering as they walk away. "We go to work every day, risking our lives, and this *jackass* shows up in a food truck with no food."

Scruff must be able to hear him, too, because he starts to laugh so hard that he has to use my serving counter to keep from falling to the ground.

When he is finally able to get himself under control, he wipes a thumb over the corners of his eyes and slaps the side of the truck. "I think we've tapped out the info from this spot. What do you say I buy you a beer? You're driving though."

"Sure. I could use a drink," I say, looking around for a car or a bike or some sort of transportation that Scruff might have used to get here. *Or a moped. He looks like the kind of guy that would ride a moped.* But I don't see anything other than my food truck and the few police cruisers on the other side of the tape.

9

After a few beers, Scruff doesn't seem quite as crazy.

And a couple of shots after that, he actually starts to make a lot of sense.

"So where do they take all these abductees?" I ask, slamming another empty shot glass on the bar.

"That's the one thing I haven't figured out yet."

I raise my hand to get the bartender's attention. When he looks at me I hold up two fingers and tap the counter.

"Okay, fine, but why do they need them?"

"I'm not sure. But I know it's an important part of their plan."

"And their plan is . . . what exactly?"

"I don't know that either."

The bartender sets down two more shots of vodka in front of us. I take mine but Scruff waves it off.

"I think I've hit my limit," he says.

So I take the second shot, too.

"Let me get this straight. You say you know the truth?"

"Uh-huh."

"But you don't know where?"

"Yes."

"Or what, or why?"

"Correct."

"So what is this truth that you claim to know?"

"Well . . . that they exist. And they're here. And if we don't do anything to stop them, they will have their way with our planet."

"Whatever you say, Scruff."

I catch the bartender's attention again, this time making a little checkmark in the air with my hand. He closes out our tab and brings my credit card back to me.

"How can you say that?" Scruff grabs my shoulder and spins my chair so that I'm facing him. "Those things took your family. Don't you even care about what happened to them?"

"Of course I care. But I don't think it matters." I slip the card back into my wallet—not forgetting that I ended up paying for both of us after he offered to buy me a drink—and take a slip of paper out of my billfold. I hand Anna's note to Scruff. "They were leaving either way."

"You can't honestly believe that still matters." He crumples the paper into a ball and throws it at the mirror behind the bar.

"Hey!"

"Mikey, listen—"

"Don't call me that," I say, my hand closing into a fist.

"Sorry, sorry." Scruff holds his hands up, palms facing me, and scoots back half a foot. "Michael, if

54

you come work with me, if we find them, you'll be a hero. She'll forget all about that little note." He lowers his hands and slowly places them on top of mine. "What do you say?"

"Sure. What the hell? Not like I've got anything better to do."

We drive back to the scene of the AMBER Alert. The police are gone. So is the tape.

"You want me to stop so we can check it out?" I ask him.

"Nah. There's nothing to find. There never is. That's me up there."

Scruff's mode of transportation isn't a moped. It's a thirty-four-foot motorhome that has clearly seen better days.

"Please don't tell me you *live* in that thing."

"Give me some credit. I have an apartment. Or . . . I did. Haven't been to it in almost a year. So maybe I don't." Scruff shrugs. "It gets the job done."

I pull over behind his RV and turn off my engine. Scruff gets out of the food truck and starts digging around in his pocket. I hear some loose change drop to the street. He holds his hand up close to his face and squints at it. He moves around some chip crumbs and candy wrappers—and I'm pretty sure he's holding the last bite of a sandwich, too—and picks up a key. Then he shoves every-thing else back into his pocket.

What am I doing?

Scruff drops the key twice before finally unlock-ing the door.

I step into the RV right behind him and can hardly believe what I see.

It's nothing like I expected. No clutter, no trash or old food littered around the floor.

A long, skinny table lines the wall across from the door. On it sits two laptops, a CB radio, a large map dotted with red pushpins, and a small filing cabinet with a padlock attached to the handle.

A corkboard hangs from the back of the dri-ver's seat headrest with another map and several sketches pinned to it.

"Wow," I say. I have no other words.

Scruff spends the better part of an hour explain-ing his research and evidence to me. Nothing concrete, but added all together, it sounds pretty damn convincing. He probably would keep going all night if I let him. And I'm tempted to. Until I get a closer look at one of the sketches on his corkboard.

"What . . . what's this?" I ask, swallowing hard. The drawing is identical to the aliens I served in my dream. And to what I thought I saw when the cop walked up to my truck earlier.

"What's it look like, Einstein? It's an alien. Haven't you been listening to anything? It's all about the aliens."

"But wh-where did this drawing come from?" My throat is dry. Each syllable, a razor blade slicing my tonsils.

"Near a military base in . . . let's see. Where was it?" Scruff takes the map off the corkboard and starts flipping pages. Apparently, it was more than one map. "Ahh. Right here." He shoves the stack of papers into my hands and pokes the center of the one on top repeatedly. "A military base in Nevada. Middle of the desert. Barely anything within fifty miles of the place."

All of a sudden, I can swallow just fine. "Area 51? Really? That's a bit cliché, isn't it?"

"It would be . . . if that's where it was."

"So there's another alien-themed base in the same state? I don't buy it."

"No, no. Area 51 is nothing. Experimental weapons and aircraft. Just like they say. But when the public got all crazy about it back in the nineties, the government helped spread the false story. It's the perfect red herring. Everyone focuses on Area 51 and ignores the base right down the road that actually *does* deal with the aliens."

"Okay, so . . . this?" I point at the sketch again before Scruff goes completely off-track.

"Right. Some old lady saw that thing walking out of the gas station a few miles from the base. I tried to investigate, but they won't let me get anywhere close to the fence with my motorhome."

"Is that really what they look like?" I can't believe I'm asking this question. I've never believed that aliens exist. But if someone saw the same thing I dreamed about, that I *saw*, wouldn't they have to be real?

"Something you want to tell me?" Scruff arches an eyebrow, like he can read my thoughts.

I purse my lips and shake my head slowly. I'm not ready to go down that rabbit hole. Not yet. "Just think it looks pretty realistic."

10

It doesn't take long before Scruff gets an idea.

"Hey," he says, "if you come with me, I bet they'd let us park your food truck close to the base. Everybody's gotta eat, right?"

"I don't know. I haven't been in much of a cooking mood lately."

"How about finding your wife and kid? Are you in *that* mood?"

He's got a point. And even though I want to say no—he doesn't seem so crazy now that I've gotten to know him, but a cross-country road trip is a lot—my curiosity is already gnawing at me.

Scruff gathers a few things from the table and carries them to the food truck.

I wait until he is outside before pulling the alien sketch off the corkboard, folding it, and slipping it into my pocket.

It's already a quarter to two in the morning when I start driving, but we couldn't stay parked next to the crime scene.

Two semi-drunk guys in a beat-up motorhome and a food truck with no food sleeping on the side of the road right where a little girl and her mother went missing less than a day ago . . . it wouldn't matter that the crime scene tape was gone. They'd lock us up for sure.

We haven't discussed what our plan is or what route to take, but I know Nevada is west of us. For tonight, that seems like enough, so I pull onto the freeway headed in that direction.

"I think I remember passing a rest stop not too far from here on my way into town," I say.

Scruff answers by gagging on saliva, shifting in his seat, and starting to snore.

"Good talk."

I turn my attention back to the empty road and watch for the sign.

A couple of long-haul drivers are parked at the rest stop, but for the most part, we have the place to ourselves.

Scruff doesn't wake up when I turn off the engine.

I take the keys with me and head for the toilets. As soon as I see my reflection in the scratched-up mirror hanging over the sink, I wish I hadn't left the house in such a rush. A few more days on the road and Scruff won't be the only one who looks like a homeless crackpot.

Who knows? Maybe that's exactly what I am.

Anna's parents paid for our house. I never thought to check the deed, but if it's in their names, I doubt they'd let me keep it. Anna was the only reason they tolerated me. Without her to keep their hatred in check, I'm screwed. Especially since they blame me for whatever happened to her and Mikey.

And as far as being a crackpot? Well . . . I'm on my way to stake out a military compound with a guy I just met. Oh, and I'm having dreams and hallucinating about aliens. So there's that.

Maybe Scruff and I aren't as different as I thought.

I turn on the sink and let the water run for a minute, hoping it will get warm.

It doesn't.

I splash it on my face anyway and then run a wet finger over my teeth. Not the same as a toothbrush, but it gets rid of some of the grime. And the aftertaste of beer and vodka.

When I get back to the truck, Scruff still hasn't moved. If it weren't for his snoring, I might think he died on me.

The driver's seat doesn't recline all the way, but I lean it back as far as I can and close my eyes.

It turns out washing my face with cold water in the middle of the night was a mistake. I'm wide awake.

With a sigh, I take Scruff's sketch out of my pocket and unfold it.

It really is uncanny how much it looks like that cop earlier. Except this one doesn't have a mustache.

After a few minutes of staring at the drawing, my eyes begin to feel heavy. Refolding the paper, I snort out a laugh and shake my head.

"Aliens," I say as my hand slides the picture into my back pocket next to my wallet. "I *must* be crazy."

I'm in the middle of a desert.

There are no buildings anywhere within sight.

The road is covered with at least an inch of sand.

And my only thought is that this is the spot to open up for the day.

I shift into park and walk into the back of the truck.

I turn the crank to open the serving window and slip my apron over my head.

Nothing but sand outside the truck.

Still, I turn around to start heating oil in the woks.

When I look out the window again, a crowd has gathered outside, all wearing military uniforms.

Except for my father-in-law.

"It's still a stupid name for a food truck," Mike says. "But there's nowhere else to eat around here."

I smile at him and open the cooler to get the meat for his order.

"Good to see you, too, Mike," I say as I break off a chunk of leg to slice. I shake it over the open cooler, letting the gold ankle bracelet I bought Anna for our first anniversary drop onto the ice before I close the lid.

After I add the meat to the rest of his order, I don't put any seasoning in the sauce. Just sesame oil. I want Mike to experience the natural flavor of his daughter's calf.

The bowl is still sizzling when I top it with noodles and hand it through the window.

"Enjoy, *Dad*," I say.

Mike takes his food and disappears into the desert. The wind has picked up and sand blocks anything farther than thirty feet from the food truck like a thick blanket of fog.

One of the aliens—a green-skinned one—steps up to order next. Its mouth-hole is surrounded by a long, frizzy beard and it is wearing a black shirt that loudly claims to know the truth.

"Not to sound racist, but that guy looked weird, right?" Alien-Scruff says.

With a smirk, I turn around to make his order.

Sitting on the stovetop where my woks should be, is that guy from the History Channel.

He brings his hands up in front of his face, raises an eyebrow, and says, "Aliens."

I wake up screaming.

When I finally remember where I am—at a rest stop in my food truck—I take a few deep breaths to try to center myself.

As my heart begins to slow down, I remember Scruff.

I roll onto my hip to look toward the passenger seat.

"Sorry about—" The seat is empty. I push myself up and crane my neck. The back of the truck is empty, too. "Scruff?"

No one else is in the parking lot, either.

The sun beats down on the pavement. I have to squint against the brightness of the morning. My food truck is the only car in the lot. There's no sign of anyone else at the rest stop. The truckers who were here when we arrived are long gone.

I pull myself back into the cab of the truck, beginning to wonder if I really am crazy. *Did I make this whole thing up?* There's no secret military base in Nevada (other than the one everybody already knows about). There's no big conspiracy behind what happened to Anna and Mikey. People go missing all the time. It doesn't mean aliens are behind it. Hell, they aren't even real. And there's no Scruff.

Except . . .

There is a pile of papers and maps on the floor in front of the passenger seat. When I see them, I check my pockets. Tucked between my wallet and the denim is a folded sheet of paper.

Unfolding it, I see the sketch that looks exactly like the customers—

aliens

—from my dream.

A knot at the base of my skull tightens. My hands are slick with sweat. My heartbeat, that had finally returned to a normal pace, starts to race.

"Hey, he's up."

I'm not proud, but a shriek slips past my lips at the sound of Scruff's voice.

He laughs.

His beard is slightly less frizzy than usual. His greasy hair is wet, slicked back away from his face. He went into the restroom to wash up. I'm not crazy. Well, not *totally* crazy.

"Ready to hit the road? If we make good time, we could be there by tomorrow night."

11

Two days later, we cross the Nevada state line.

"Almost there," I tell Scruff. "But you never told me what our plan is once we get there."

"Isn't it obvious? You open your truck. Everybody's gotta eat."

"No, no, no. I told you, I'm done with cooking. I can't do it anymore."

"You're going to have to. And it's going to have to be good. That is, if we want to get close enough to learn anything."

"I . . . I don't think I can," I say, my voice fading to a whimper. This is the first time I've even considered cooking since I learned about Anna and Mikey and the thought makes me want to head straight back to the garage with the dryer hose.

"Plus, think about it," Scruff continues, either not able to hear my protest or simply ignoring it, "people who work with food are damn-near invisible. We get lucky and the right couple of guys stop by, they might tell us everything we need to know just by bitching about work to each other. Whoa! Hey, hey, hey, turn here."

Scruff is working as our navigator. We pulled up directions on my phone, but I had to turn the volume off when Mike's messages wouldn't stop coming. If the things he keeps saying and accusing me of didn't ring true, I'd probably block his number. I think I need the constant reminders, though. Of Anna and Mikey. And everything I should have done differently. Besides, there's always the chance that they will show up at her parent's house. And I have to at least hope Mike would tell me if that happens.

"I hope it's like riding a bike," Scruff says, pulling me away from my thoughts.

"Yeah. Wait, what?"

"Cooking. I hope it's like riding a bike. Because if they don't like your food, we're screwed. I sure as hell can't cook."

"I don't have anything to make."

"Looks like we have a stop to make then." Scruff grabs my phone and searches for a Costco, or something similar, on the way to the base.

We leave my phone in the truck when we go into the store.

By the time we get back, there is a new message from Mike. And two missed calls from an unknown number.

The phone starts to ring while I am loading the two carts of food into my coolers.

Scruff looks at the screen.

"It's that same number again. You want it?" He holds the phone out toward me.

I shake my head and keep working. "It's just my father-in-law. Probably using someone else's phone to trick me into answering so he can blame me for everything again."

I slam the lid onto a cooler and take the empty shopping carts back to the front of the store.

My phone beeps when I get back.

"You sure?" Scruff asks as I climb into my seat. "They left a voicemail."

I take the phone from him and tap on the notification.

It isn't from Mike.

"Mr. Morley," a voice I don't recognize says. Whoever it is clears their throat and starts over. "Mr. Morley, this is Detective Jones. I know someone has already spoken with you about the potential abduction of your wife and son—"

I close my eyes and see the History Channel guy talking with his hands. *Aliens.*

"—we've received some calls that have us looking into a different angle. If you could swing by the station this afternoon or give me a call back at—"

I hang up before the detective can give me his number. I'm not calling back. There is no other angle. It's all Mike. He must be calling the police station. Telling them the same things he's been sending to me. *It's all Michael's fault. He did this to them. It's his fault they are gone.*

I must not be hiding my emotions very well.

Less than two minutes after pulling out of the parking lot, Scruff turns his head and stares at me.

"What?" I snap, sounding harsher than I mean to.

"You good, man?"

I let go of the steering wheel to run my hands up my face and through my hair.

"I don't actually know." I sigh, grabbing the wheel quickly before the upcoming curve in the road. "I don't think I am."

"Is that why you stole the sketch from my RV?"

My mouth snaps shut.

"It's all right. I don't mind. As long as you give it back when you're done. What'd you take it for, anyway?"

I focus on the road, unsure of what I should tell him.

After about a mile, I look at Scruff. He's looking at me again. Or he's been watching me the whole time, waiting for an answer.

"I've been having this dream . . ." I tell him everything I can remember about each version of the dream that I've had.

"That sounds just like, hold on, I think I have it here." Scruff unbuckles his seatbelt and crawls to the back of the truck where the stack of papers he brought is. He flips through them until he finds what he is looking for. "I met an old lady a few years back. She had this recurring dream where she was on a large platter in the middle of her dining table. It was always Thanksgiving and her entire family sat around the table, except they were all aliens. Her kids and grandkids all waited with silverware in their hands while her husband stood over her with their electric carving knife. She said he would always ask who wanted the dark meat before slicing off a chunk of her thigh and passing it around the table."

The image of an old lady as a Thanksgiving turkey makes me laugh even if the similarities to my dreams are enough to churn my stomach.

"That's only part of it, though," I say. "If it was just the dream, I probably would have written it off as a coincidence. That last crime scene we were at . . . the cop that tried to order something . . . he looked just like this." I take the folded-up picture out of my pocket and give it back to Scruff.

Now he's the one that is speechless.

"Well?" I say after his mouth has been hanging open for a minute and a half.

"You saw one?"

"Yeah. Or I thought I did. Just for a second. Then he looked normal. But it was weird that I thought he looked like the things in my dream. And then I saw the sketch. I don't know what came over me. I just took it."

"You saw one?"

I think my story broke Scruff because that's all he says for an hour.

"I think we're here," I tell Scruff.

I turned off the main road twelve miles ago and haven't seen anything but sand since. Until now.

Maybe three-quarters of a mile ahead of us is a tall, thick fence. Barbed wire swirls on top and all.

There's something strange, though.

Behind the fence is a dusty field. And in the middle is a giant billboard.

The billboard has one word written on it:
HAY!

It even has an exclamation point.

As we get closer, I can see more of the field. Round hay bales are everywhere, tightly wrapped with that white plastic that makes them look like giant marshmallows.

What sort of secret military base sells hay?

Another half mile down the road is a gate.

I pull over and park in front of it.

"Now what?"

"Now, it's time to get to work," Scruff says. Apparently he's moved past the shock of my revelation—if that's really what it was. The farther away from that crime scene I get, the more I start to think I might have overreacted to something I imagined. Stress does that to people, right? And I've certainly had plenty of *that* in the last month.

"I still don't think they are going to let us stay," I say, washing my hands and slipping my apron over my head.

Scruff cranks open the serving window and by the time I turn around, there are already two people waiting. *Maybe they will.*

"You can't be here," one of them says. They must have walked over from the guard shack next to the gate after I turned off the engine.

The other one unbuttons the strap holding his gun in the holster on his hip.

Without thinking, I put my hands up.

Not Scruff.

"Oh, come on," he says. "You guys have to eat, right? What's the harm in letting us park outside? We're gonna be with the truck the whole time, and even if we wanted to try anything, you're sitting right by the gate."

The soldier with his hand on his gun relaxes.

The other guy looks at Scruff's face, considering, and I'm pretty sure his eyes dart down long enough to read Scruff's shirt.

"All right," he says. "Just for today. But if the food sucks, you're outta here."

It's too early for lunch, so I'm surprised when they want to order right away.

Scruff grabs his stack of papers and slips back up into the passenger seat while I start cooking.

When I open the cooler to get the meat, part of me is expecting to see Anna's leg, or Mikey's arm.

It's just pork, though.

"Shit. Oh, shit. Holy shit, I gotta go." Scruff has my phone in his hands. He takes it with him when he opens the door and jumps out.

I start to follow him but one of the soldiers pounds on the side of my truck.

"This going to take much longer? We do have jobs to get back to."

"Right. Sorry," I say, dropping the pork into the woks with their veggies.

I turn back around to get the sauces ready and realize I forgot to get everything I would normally use to make them while we were at the store.

I check the shelves, frantically searching for enough of anything to season their food with.

All I manage to find is a jug full of sesame oil and a large container of ground coriander.

"This is going to be interesting," I mutter as I mix together the simplest sauce I've ever made.

Handing the bowls through the window, I watch as the soldiers sniff their stir-fry. At almost the exact same time, they twirl some of the noodles onto their forks and raise them to their mouths.

Scruff is going to be pissed, I think. *Oh well, if he wants this so badly, maybe he should be here to help.*

Right on cue, Scruff walks up behind the soldiers.

"Well, gentlemen, what's the verdict?"

"Not bad," says the one who had been ready to pull his gun on us.

"Yeah," says the other through a mouthful of noodles. He looks up at me. "What's your secret?"

I shrug. "Just a shit-ton of coriander."

They both laugh as they head back toward the shack near the gate.

"Not bad for someone who isn't in a cooking mood. Nice work," Scruff says, handing my phone to me through the window. "Looks like you're good here. I have something I need to go check out. It might take me a day or two, but I'll be back."

"You can't be serious. Coming here was your brilliant idea. What do you expect me to do without you?"

"Make them food and don't give them a reason to make you leave. I wouldn't go if it wasn't important."

A cab pulls up behind the food truck. Scruff runs toward it.

"Trust me," he says as he ducks into the backseat and leaves me alone in the middle of the Nevada desert.

12

Over the course of the day, word must spread throughout the base about my food truck.

I never seem to have a line, but as soon as I hand one order out the window, someone is standing there ready to place another.

Not all that long ago, a day like this would have flown by. I'd have felt energized by it. A wave of electricity holding a smile on my face and leaving me buzzing until at least the next morning.

But not today.

Today, it takes everything I have not to close the window and drive back across the country. To hell with Scruff and whatever he thinks is important enough to leave me here alone.

I try to make conversation with a few of the soldiers, but no one says much of anything.

They all seem to be big fans of my terrible, coriander-only sauce, though.

Anna always used to say I could take a flattened squirrel from the side of the road and make it taste like a gourmet meal. That was before I told her about my dream—owning a food truck, not serving stir-fried slices of her body to aliens—but the memory takes the edge off of the feeling of abandonment Scruff left me with.

At around two in the afternoon, a pair of soldiers walk through the gate toward my truck.

"You must be the cook that nobody can stop talking about," one of them says. He looks Hispanic but has no accent as far as I can tell. Like all the others, he has a close-cropped haircut and is wearing tan and green fatigues. Although, unlike the others, he left the top button undone. At the base of his neck, running along the V-neck collar of his white undershirt, is a jagged purple scar.

I lean forward through the window and pretend to look around. "I suppose I must. I don't see any other cooks around here." It is honestly painful to keep a smile on my face as I say the words.

Neither of the soldiers even smirk at my joke attempt. I know it was a corny thing to say, and I've never been accused of being funny before, but I had hoped to at least get a courtesy chuckle or something. Maybe I'll leave Scruff on his own to make small talk with a bunch of soldiers with sticks up their asses for a while when he gets back. Whenever *that* might be.

"We'll take two," the Hispanic soldier says, holding up two fingers in case I misheard him.

The other soldier grabs his arm and pulls it down. "Not so fast," he says. He takes another step toward the truck and looks around inside. "Who is your supplier? We like to know where our food is coming from around here."

I clear my throat. "Well . . . I'm not usually in the area, so I don't have one nearby." I stop short of admitting that everything in the truck came from a grocery store. "You don't happen to know of one, do you?"

"I'll ask around," he says, not impressed.

The first soldier looks at him and then back at me. He brings his hand up again, with only the index finger raised this time. "Sounds like it'll just be one bowl."

Right before sunset, there is still no sign of Scruff.

What I do see is an officer—I don't know much about the military, but it's clear that this guy is pretty high up the food chain—coming toward me.

Instead of fatigues like all the others, he has on a blue suit covered with medals. He is carrying a clipboard in one hand while his other holds a hat beneath his arm.

His hair is longer than everyone else's, too, and glued to his head with product.

When he reaches the serving window, he doesn't order anything. He sets the clipboard down and waits.

"Can I get you something to eat?" My voice trembles even though he is just standing there.

He nods toward the clipboard. "A requisition form. It has been brought to my attention that many of my soldiers have taken a liking to your food. If you are to continue serving this base, we need to know that you are using quality ingredients."

The gulp when I swallow is loud enough that there is no way he doesn't hear it. "Did someone have an issue with the quality of my food?"

The creases on my forehead prickle with sweat and start to itch. Despite losing all desire to cook, my pride still exists. And it bruises easily.

"Not that I am aware of," the officer says. "However, they would like me to request that you stay. In order for me to allow that, you have to fill out the requisition form."

As I finish filling out the form on the clipboard, three more soldiers arrive at the window. They were laughing and smiling as they came through the gate, but when they get near the officer, their faces are all emotionless. They snap to attention and salute him.

He returns their salute and gives me a half-nod as he takes the clipboard from me.

No one moves—including me—until he is back on the base with the gate closed behind him.

The soldiers go back to whatever conversation they were having on their way to the truck while I make their dinners.

Scruff would want me to eavesdrop, but I'm too exhausted to worry about that. A steady stream of customers all day will do that to a guy. Especially when that guy has barely gotten out of bed for the past month.

The guilt of missing a potential opportunity to gather information eats at me as I cook. This is the best chance I've had all day to learn something and I'm not even giving it a shot.

As I pass the three bowls through the window, they stop talking. I try to think of something to ask them that won't seem too suspicious. I draw a blank until I spot the billboard in the field behind the fence.

"So, what's the deal with all the hay? What are you guys, like, government farmers or something?"

The three soldiers all look at me, their mouths straight, eyes narrowed.

And then they turn toward each other and burst into laughter.

"Yeah," one of them says, elbowing both of the others playfully. "We're farmers."

They take their bowls and return to base, looking over their shoulders at me a few times, still laughing until they are out of sight.

13

I close the serving window as soon as the lights above the fence turn on. By now, I'm pretty sure that I've served everyone who works on the base today. Even if there's anyone left who wants to get food from me, I'm damn-near out of everything until whenever the stuff on that requisition form shows up. Seems like as good a time as any to call it a night.

When I finish washing everything, I hang up my apron and crawl into the passenger seat. Scruff still isn't back—if he's even coming back—and after the day I've had, I want to be able to stretch out without banging my crotch into the steering wheel.

My body aches all over, but I can't keep my eyes closed. Too many questions.

Where the hell is Scruff?

What are all these people doing on the other side of the fence?

Why do I have to order my food with one of their forms?

Do they let people buy that hay or is the sign just to tell people that it's there?

How is any of this even remotely connected to Anna and Mikey?

Are they okay?

Are they even still alive?

I give up trying to sleep and reach for my phone on the dashboard. The battery is almost dead and I have no way to charge it, so I don't open any apps. I quickly scroll through the notifications hoping to see something from Scruff. Nothing. Just a bunch of text messages and missed calls from Mike, and a couple of voicemails from that detective that wants to talk to me. I'm not surprised. I don't think Scruff even has a phone. And if he does, I never gave him my number.

I turn off the phone to save the little battery that's left and reach up to click on a light.

After a quick look around the truck, I turn off the light. I didn't bring a single thing with me except for what was in my pockets when I tried to kill myself, and Scruff took his entire stack of papers with him when he left.

I open the door and step out into the cool night air. I haven't been out of the truck all day, so I take a deep breath hoping the fresh air will help calm my mind. That is a mistake. The wind is blowing and dozens (maybe hundreds) of grains of coarse desert sand scratch the insides of my nostrils. I feel the grit all the way into my sinuses. It makes me sneeze.

At the sound of my sneeze, a spotlight attached to the guard building lights up, aimed directly at me.

A muffled voice blasts from a loudspeaker.

"You are not authorized to be out of your vehicle. Return to the food truck immediately or we will be forced to remove you from the area."

So much for clearing my head . . .

I wake up in the morning when the sun reflects just right off the side mirror into my eyes. I have no idea what time I finally managed to fall asleep, but however long I slept for doesn't feel like enough.

Squinting hard against the sunlight, I reach toward the steering wheel and turn the key to light up the clock on the dashboard. When I see that it's still far too early for anyone to want stir-fry, I turn the key back and roll over away from the glare.

Before I'm able to fall back asleep, someone pounds on the back of my truck.

I ignore it, hoping whoever it is will go away.

They knock again.

"All right, all right," I groan, opening the door and rolling out of the truck. Two soldiers watch me struggle to my feet. One presses the lever on a pallet jack to drop off the food I requested. A lot of it. The other hands me a clipboard.

"Need a signature," he says.

"Yeah, yeah." I yawn and rub the back of my neck as I take a pen from him.

He points to an X on the bottom of the page.

In my half-aware state, I scribble something that looks nothing like my actual signature. He takes the pen back and pulls a copy of the requisition form for me off the clipboard.

"If you don't mind me asking, how'd you manage to get such a big order so fast?"

"We do mind," says the guy with the pallet jack. "And you should focus on making the food. We will handle the rest."

"Whoa, jackpot!" Scruff shouts as he pulls himself out of the backseat of a cab that parks behind the food truck. The soldiers turn toward Scruff and exchange a quizzical look. He runs over to me and looks up at the sky. "It's starting to warm up out here. Let's get this into the truck before it goes bad." They ignore him once they see that he is with me and head back to the base.

The idea of the food spoiling gives me a flashback to the rotting boxes that sat on my porch while I stayed in bed for weeks. The memory makes my nose sting.

"Where have you been?" I say, sounding more like a mom or jealous girlfriend than a random guy he barely knows.

"Not out here," Scruff whispers. "They're listening."

"Tell me what's going on," I say as soon as the last box is inside the food truck and the door is closed behind me. "What was so important that you had to take off with no explanation?"

"It's all right here," Scruff says, tapping a new notebook on the top of his stack of papers.

"I've got boxes to unload. Explain it to me."

"I used your phone to check one of my message boards. Someone posted that they'd been held captive on a military base in Nevada. He managed to escape, and he has evidence of large-scale alien experiments backed by the U.S. government."

"What's your point? I thought we were looking for my wife and son, not trying to uncover a conspiracy."

"Do I really have to spell it out for you? It's here. This base. That's where he escaped from. Where the experiments are happening."

"So what? That doesn't help me."

"Of course it does! What do you think they took your family for? They aren't on vacation, I can tell you that for sure."

Once again, Scruff is making a lot of sense. "Okay, so you talked to this guy. What's next?"

"That depends. What did you find out while I was gone?"

Scruff is not impressed with my intelligence gathering skills.

"Hay? You actually had a chance to ask them a direct question, and you asked about hay?"

"Hey, you're the one who left me here, remember? This is your world, not mine. I don't know what I'm supposed to ask."

"All right, fine. It's fine. I think I got enough for us to go on. We can go over everything tonight.

Until then, why don't you stick to cooking and let me handle the questions."

If I thought yesterday was a long day, today is even longer. I was *way* off when I thought I'd served most everybody on base. That explains the size of the order they dropped off this morning, though.

Scruff doesn't ask the soldiers any questions. At least, none that I can hear. But he told me to focus on cooking, so that's what I'm trying to do.

I open the cooler and cut open a bag of meat. I'm not entirely sure what type of meat it is, but it's all the same. And it's pre-sliced.

When I drop a handful into my wok, it sizzles and lets off a smell that I can't quite place. It smells gray. I don't know if that makes any sense, but that's what it smells like. Anywhere else, I would throw out the whole cooler and get some- thing more recognizable. And fresher.

But here at the base, this is what they want me to cook. Who am I to disagree?

When the sun sets, Scruff closes the serving window for me. He starts telling me his plan while I wash dishes.

He takes a new map out of the middle of the notebook.

"The base is too big to explore all in one night. Even if we didn't have to avoid security. Which we do." Scruff pulls a marker out of his pocket. He places a black dot on the top of the map. "This is where we are." Then he puts an X on the bottom left corner. "And this is where my source escaped from. If they haven't found the breach in the fence yet, we should be able to start tonight."

"Good luck with that," I say. "I tried getting out of the truck for a little air last night and they had a spotlight on me within seconds. There's no way to get out without them seeing the doors open."

"Wanna bet?" Scruff says with a wink.

14

I had no idea that my food truck has a panel on the floor that can be removed. But somehow, Scruff knows about it.

Within ten minutes, we are both lying flat on our bellies beneath the truck.

He taps my side with his hand.

"Told you. Now scoot toward the back of the truck. But make sure you don't stand up once you're out."

I nod and start inching my way backward. Scruff does the same.

Once we are clear of the food truck, we stay on the ground, moving farther away from the gate and keeping the truck between us and the guard building at all times.

"All right, this should be far enough." He sounds like he's done this before. For all I know, he has.

We stay between a quarter and a half mile away from the fence as we move toward the X on Scruff's map.

Even though we are only walking, my heart might as well be running a marathon. All this sneaking around is exhilarating, and we aren't even to the risky part yet.

It takes almost two hours to reach the spot we are looking for. There are no lights near this part of the fence. Nobody patrolling the perimeter. No spotlights or megaphones or guns.

Only me and my fearless leader, and hopefully a hole in the fence.

It doesn't take long to find the hole. Whoever told Scruff about it made sure that he knew what landmarks to look for to be able to find it in the dark.

And no one on the other side of the fence has found it yet. As long as we don't get caught, they probably won't.

"This way," Scruff whispers once we are through. He wants me to follow him to one of the large buildings.

I'm more curious about the hay bales. There are so many of them. And we're so close.

"Just a second," I say. "Something's bugging me. I just want to see if there's something special about this hay."

I hear Scruff groan, but when I look over my shoulder, he is following me.

I have no idea what I'm looking for, or why I think I'll even be able to tell if it's anything other than plain old hay. I'm not a farmer. The only time I've ever even seen hay up close is when Anna made us take family pictures sitting on a bale at the pumpkin patch.

When I get to the closest bale, I grab a handful of plastic and pull as hard as I can.

"Be careful," Scruff hisses. "We can't leave any signs that we were here. Not if we want to ever get in again."

I nod but ignore him and rip the plastic.

When the tear is big enough to see into, I freeze.

I may not be an expert, but I don't have to be to know that this isn't an ordinary bale of hay.

It's not hay at all.

It's a person.

I clap both hands to my mouth to stifle my scream. When Scruff sees my reaction, he practically throws me out of the way so he can see.

"Oh. My. God." His reaction is a bit more controlled. He still brings a hand—just one, though—up to his mouth, but he does it slowly. And without screaming into it.

"How . . . how are you still standing there looking at it? What the *fuck* is going on here? That's a person in there!"

"It's not just any person. That sketch you pocketed from my RV . . . she's the one who drew it."

I double over and vomit between my legs. So much for not leaving a trace.

Wiping my mouth with the back of my hand as I stand up, it hits me. There has got to be at least a hundred more of these hay bales. Could there be a person in each one?

"Could there—" I start to ask Scruff, but he doesn't let me finish.

"I think so. Most likely."

As soon as he agrees with me, I sprint toward the next closest one and tear at the plastic.

Inside this one is a teenage boy with what looks like the first hint of a mustache.

I run to another.

A young girl. Can't be more than seven or eight years old.

And another.

This one looks about my age. It's hard to tell because his cheeks are covered with open sores. Bright red and oozing pus. His skin looks darker than mine. Mexican, maybe? Unlike the others, his eyes are open. Unmoving, but open. And pointed right at me. It's hard to look away, but I can't take it anymore. There is absolutely zero life behind those eyes. Like a doll's eyes. Unnatural.

A sudden urge comes over me. I need to get him out. Get them all out, eventually. But he's first. I grab onto the ripped plastic with both hands and let my body weight drop. The plastic rips, but not as much as I hoped it would, so I stand back up.

I can hear Scruff's wheezing breath coming up behind me.

He puts a hand on my shoulder. "I think we better call it a night. We'll come back tomorrow after dark."

"Yeah," I say, looking up at the horizon. Already, the midnight blue of the night is starting to take on a pinkish hue. "Yeah, you're right."

I tug on the plastic that I'm still holding one last time. It stretches enough to reveal the shoulders of the man trapped inside. He doesn't have a shirt on. His shoulders, chest, and neck are covered with more of those sores.

And his neck ... At the base of his neck, running at a sharp angle toward the center of his chest, is a jagged purple scar that looks like an old knife wound.

"Wait," I say to Scruff, who is tugging on my arm, trying to pull me back toward the hole in the fence. "I know him. He's one of the soldiers I served yesterday."

We don't talk at all on the way back to the food truck. Or when we crawl underneath and through the open floor panel.

Scruff puts the panel back in place once we are inside, in case anyone happens to be able to see the floor through the serving window tomorrow.

How in the hell are we supposed to make it through tomorrow after what we found?

And that's just outside. What else might we find *inside* one of the buildings?

The thought sends a chill throughout my entire body.

Safely back inside the food truck, I thought for sure that Scruff would have something to say.

He doesn't.

15

I have that dream again.

Much of it is the same as usual.

I'm working in the food truck.

There's a hungry crowd waiting for food.

I run out of meat and have to get more from the cooler.

But this time, there are no body parts waiting to be sliced.

Anna and Mikey are pre-sliced into thin round chunks of meat.

I know it is them because of the accessories still stuck to the meat (the engagement ring I gave Anna that I got on sale at the mall before all the stores went out of business, and a silicone wristband with a smiley face on it that Mikey refuses to take off).

When I drop the pre-sliced meat into the wok, it makes the entire truck smell gray.

Now it's time to make the sauce.

I don't have my usual ingredients, so I look around for something to improvise with.

I find it beneath the meat in the cooler.

The head of the Hispanic soldier with the scar.

With the biggest spoon I have, I scoop some of the pus out of the sores on his cheeks.

I add it to the sesame oil and mix until all the clumps are gone.

Then I drizzle it over the stir-fry and hand it out the window.

The entire crowd surrounding my truck is made up of the soldiers from the base.

Scruff has been up front in the driver's seat the entire time.

When he sees the soldier who reaches for the food, he waves me closer to him.

I lean close enough to hear him whisper.

"I don't want to sound like a racist, but these soldiers shouldn't look like this, should they?"

I step up to the window to get a better look at my customers.

A head pops into view above the counter, much closer than I expected anyone to be.

The face is familiar, and the hair on top of the head is wild and unkempt.

After his head appears in my field of vision, this guy reaches up to slap the serving counter with both hands.

"Aliens."

I decide to keep the dream to myself. And the longer into the day we get, the more I'm convinced that I made the right decision.

I'm managing fairly well, all things considered.

Then again, I've always had a knack for shutting off my emotions. Especially when I'm around other people.

The day actually seems to go by pretty quickly.

Maybe not for Scruff. He's shaking and his hands stay balled into fists all day.

By the time we close the serving window, he seems a little more like himself.

Enough to share a plan with me, at least.

"We have to ignore the hay bales tonight."

"Are you crazy? We have to help those people."

"Michael, we don't even know if they can be helped. There's no way to know what was done to them before they got wrapped up. And didn't you notice when our Hispanic friend stopped by for lunch? They might not even be real people in there. Maybe they're clones."

"Aliens or clones? Which is it? You have to pick a lane, Scruff."

"Could be both. We won't know unless we ignore the hay bales and check *inside* the buildings."

He's right. I know he is. But I will still check one or two more before I follow him into any building. Anna and Mikey might be in one of those bales.

We slip through the hole in the fence with no trouble. And the path to the closest building looks clear.

"Stay close and keep up," Scruff says. "Once we start moving, I won't be able to pay attention to you. I'll be making sure we stay in the clear. Ready?"

"Ready," I say, already scouting which hay bales I want to check before following him.

"Okay, let's move."

And Scruff does move. He moves fast.

I have time to get to one bale and rip it open, but by the time I can see that the person inside isn't Anna or Mikey, Scruff is already into the building. The door is swinging shut behind him.

I don't know if I'll be able to catch up.

Without even bothering to check my surroundings, I start running across the open field toward the building.

He was serious about not slowing down.

When I open the door, all I see is an empty hallway.

"Scruff?" I whisper. Then, a little louder, "Scruff, where are you?"

I think I hear the echoes of footsteps coming from the staircase at the end of the hall.

If that's the way he went, there's only one direction he could have gone.

Down.

But how far down? I grab onto the railing and lean over the edge. The staircase looks like it descends forever.

"Scruff?" I hiss into the void and immediately regret my decision

Scruff, Scruff, Scruff, Scruff.

His name bounces off the walls all the way to the bottom, wherever that is.

If he's down there, he must hear it.

But so would anyone else who happens to be near the stairs.

I stay where I am for a moment, listening. Listening and strongly considering going back to my food truck.

The sound of Mike's voice in my head might be the only reason I don't leave.

You selfish shit, I imagine him saying, *you came all this way because you think your family is here. And now that you're actually here, you want to give up because you're scared. You are worthless. No wonder she left you.*

By the time I finally reach the bottom of the stairs, I can't hear anything.

The staircase gives way to a long corridor with doors on either side every fifteen feet, each with a small window at eye level.

Scruff could be on the other side of any of them.

Or none of them.

I'm more tempted than ever to turn back.

No one has seen me yet.

I could still get out of this.

Save myself.

But then I remember what Anna wrote on that little scrap of paper.

Don't bother trying to find us until you get your priorities straight.

"No," I say, probably too loudly. "I'm not leaving. Not until I find them. And Scruff."

I lean back into the stairway and look up. It's too dark to see, but it doesn't sound like anyone is coming after me yet so I move toward the first door.

Lifting myself onto my toes to get a better view, I cup my hands over my eyes and look into the first window.

In the center of the room is a long metal table with a nude man lying face down on top of it. There are four soldiers standing around the table wearing white lab coats over their fatigues.

One of them has a long metal rod with a joint in the middle. He bends it down toward the unconscious man's ass. Pausing to turn toward the others, he smiles before shoving it in.

I can only tell he is smiling because his cheeks ball up next to the slits where his nose should be. He doesn't have a mouth. Just a small, toothless hole. And his egg-shaped eyes cover half of his face.

The others start to laugh and I catch glimpses of their faces, too.

I push myself away from the window and gesture with my hands toward the door, just like that guy on TV.

"Aliens!"

16

I stumble back, the heels of my shoes catching on the concrete floor.

I land seated in the middle of the hallway and push myself away from the door until my back is flat against the wall on the opposite side.

Several doors open.

At least one soldier sticks a head out of each to see what all the commotion is about.

And each head isn't human.

When their oversized eyes spot me, they all come into the hallway.

The door right in front of me opens and all four of the aliens I saw step out.

I'm surrounded.

I'm screwed.

They all stand around me, stand over me, but none make a move to get closer.

It's like they are waiting for something. Or someone.

The only closed door remaining swings open at the end of the hall. The officer that brought me the requisition form the other day makes his way toward me, his hat still tucked under one arm.

All of the others move out of his way as he approaches.

His skin is the same shade of blue as his uniform.

None of the others have blue skin. A lot of green and gray, but only one blue.

"Oh my God, Scruff was actually right. Area 51 *is* a cover. This is the real alien base. And—holy shit—you're *all* aliens?"

The blue officer laughs. It sounds almost like normal human laughter except for a few clicks and hums mixed in.

"Mr. Morley, correct?" His mouth hole doesn't move when he speaks and I have to tell myself he's wearing a Halloween mask to be able to respond.

"Y-y-yes."

"Come with me, please. We need to have a chat."

The officer turns around and returns to the room at the far end of the hall.

One of the alien soldiers steps forward (I think he's the one who was holding the probe) and helps me to my feet.

All of the others move out of the way so I can follow their superior officer, but none go back to what they were doing before I enter the officer's room.

"Close the door, please, Mr. Morley."

"How do you know my name?" This is the hay bale question all over again. I always ask the least important questions when I'm put on the spot. Although, given what we found inside them, maybe it wasn't such a stupid question.

"Your requisition form. You signed it when we dropped off your delivery."

"What is this place?"

"Exactly what it appears to be. It's a military base. Only it is for my military rather than yours."

"But why? What are you doing here?"

"Ahh, now you're getting to the good stuff, Mr. Morley. Ordinarily, I would kill someone before sharing this. But, I must confess, we've all become a bit addicted to your food truck. So, instead of killing you, I will offer you a deal."

The officer stands up from behind his desk and opens a door that I didn't see when I entered the room. He exits into another hallway. I don't move.

"Follow me, please," the officer says, ducking his head back into the room when he realizes I'm not following.

"Yes sir," I say, not knowing how else to respond.

He stops walking and turns to face me. "Please, call me Bob."

"Bob?" I can't hide the surprise in my voice.

"Yes. It is not my true name, but I love the way it sounds in your language. Buh-aw-buh. It's fantastic."

"Okay . . . Bob."

"Good, good. Now back to business. This is a deal that I've never offered a human before. Like I said, we can't get enough of your cooking."

"It's nothing special, I just put a shit-ton of coriander on it."

"No need to be modest here, Mr. Morley."

"I'm not, I swear. Besides, I don't even know what kind of meat I've been feeding you."

"Oh that? That's no secret. It's pod meat."

"What?"

"We'll get to it. You'll get all the answers you are looking for. Including this one." Bob opens a door and steps to the side so I can see into the small room.

Inside the room, there are two of those people-filled hay bales. But these ones aren't wrapped all the way yet. Everything from the shoulder up is still uncovered. And these bales aren't filled with just any people. It's Anna and Mikey.

I reach out my arms and step forward, but Bob closes the door.

"You can have your family back," he says. "Well, not exactly. They will never be the same as you remember them. Their personalities will be flat. Their emotions never too high or too low. But they will be alive. And you can be together. Would you like that, Mr. Morley?"

"Yes, yes, of course."

"Then they are yours. Though there are a few conditions."

Bob goes on to tell me that in order to be with them, we can't leave the base. Which is fine by him because he wants me here to make food every day.

We will be provided for and given a house, so there will be no more uncomfortable nights spent in the food truck. I will get the answers to any questions I have about them and their plans, but I can never repeat them to anyone.

"Yes, yes. I agree. Give me my family."

"There's one more thing," Bob says, still blocking the door. "We have your friend. You have to choose. Them," he nods toward the door, "who are only partially the people you remember, or him, who we have done nothing to. Yet."

"Them," I say without hesitation.

"Good. He needs to be reassimilated."

"Scruff is one of you?"

"What? Oh, I see. No, no, I assure you he is not. Perhaps I used a misleading word. English can be a tricky language. We have found it is easier to maintain our anonymity when we place certain individuals into these fanatical groups. Hand-selected plants that know enough about our operation to become influential within the groups while lacking the requisite evidence to convince the population at large. To most of the planet, they appear to be crazy despite knowing the truth. It really is the perfect cover, don't you think? But he is one hundred percent human."

Bob steps to the side and lets me reach for the door.

"Wait," I say before turning the doorknob. "What's with the hay bales?"

"Those are our pods. It's where we put them after we have run all of our tests."

"Tests? Like what those guys were doing with the probe?"

"No. Not like that. They were in the vacation room. They saved up their time off and rented it out for the weekend to burn off a little steam. Anyway, the pods allow the meat to cure until we can use it. Well, I suppose now it will be until it's ready for *you* to use. Enjoy this moment, Mr. Morley. Today is the first day of your life."

I try not to think about the pods while I open the door and rush to my family.

A few days later, we are all set up in our new house. Bob gave us time to get settled before I had to start working. Today is the day. And there are already soldiers waiting to order.

In the distance, I see someone who isn't wearing fatigues coming toward the serving window. Since the first day I parked here, I haven't served anyone who didn't work on the base.

As he gets closer, I think I recognize him. He looks different—hair is freshly washed instead of greasy, and his beard is trimmed—but I'd know that shirt anywhere. A black tee that hangs to his knees, with big white letters. *I KNOW THE TRUTH.*

It's Scruff.

I want so badly to lean through the window. To take him by the shoulders and shake. To tell him that he's right. About everything. But that would be breaking the deal.

"What's wrong, Dad?" Mikey asks, tugging on my apron. The vegetables in the wok are turning black. Smoke starts to fill up the back of the truck.

"Nothing, son." I dump the wok into the trash can and restart.

A few minutes later, I hand a couple of orders through the window.

Scruff is standing less than twenty feet away now. Waiting.

As soon as the two soldiers take their food and begin to walk back to the base, he comes up to the window.

"Hi, Sc— sir," I say, catching myself before I say his name. "How can I help you?"

"How can you do this?" *Does he remember?*

I swallow hard. "I'm sorry. What are you talking about?"

"Don't you know what they do in there? They're aliens. Or they work with the aliens. Something to do with aliens. And lying to everyone about it." He doesn't recognize me. But this is definitely the same old Scruff.

"I wouldn't know anything about that," I say, shaking my head and forcing a smile. "I just work here. Everybody's gotta eat."

I lean back and call up to Anna, who is sitting in the passenger seat.

"How about some music?"

She flips through the disc binder and puts a Styx album into the truck's CD player.

I put my arm around Mikey and watch my customers head back to the base as the music starts to play.

AUTHOR'S NOTE

It's always interesting to think back to where story ideas first come from. This one, for example, came from a throwaway comment my dad made when we drove past a field filled with marshmallow-shaped hay bales. He'd had a couple of drinks and was trying to be funny. He yelled out, "It's the pods. Watch out for the pods." As far as I know, he'd never called them that before and hasn't since, but that one line stuck with me and turned into this strange, dark, little story.

But on a more serious note, I know that I reference Michael attempting suicide in the story. Hell, I do more than that. I show him trying to kill himself. And while I felt that it was important for his character to do that, thoughts of suicide should never be taken lightly. If you or someone you know is struggling, PLEASE, PLEASE, PLEASE reach out to someone and ask for help. And if you aren't sure who to talk to, give the National Suicide Prevention Lifeline a call at 1-800-273-TALK(8255) or you can also call 988 for the Suicide & Crisis Lifeline.

Made in USA - Kendallville, IN
32953_9798988139683
12.17.2024 0007